The Most Difficult Lesson
and other stories

Precious Gift Series

Nadejda Hristova

Illustrated by Kate and Lilly Aleksovs

The Door To The Lumber Room

Once upon a time there lived a modest, hard-working man whose daughters had long been married. Only his son remained living with him, but the boy was still young; there was plenty of time for him to find a wife. Each day father and son worked together from morning to dusk. They lived simply, acquiring all they needed and were content.

Time passed and the boy grew to be a fine young man. One day the father called his son to him.

"Son, my strength is giving way and I wish to leave you with some wise counsel."

The young man sat by his father's side. "I'm listening, Father."

"When you meet a girl in whom your heart delights, before asking for her hand in marriage, I advise you to do one thing," the father spoke softly.

The son leaned forward. "Yes, Father. What is it?"

"Ask her to show you the door to the lumber room of her home."

"But Father, why?" the young man enquired.

"When young girls are waiting for guests to arrive, they clean and tidy their homes putting everything in order. But Son, no one thinks to look in the lumber room. If a girl really likes her home to be well-ordered, then the lumber room will also be clean and neat.

The father died. Before long, the young man met a girl to whom he took a fancy. Day and night he thought about her and, in due course, decided to ask for her hand in marriage. When he arrived at the young woman's house, he remembered his father's counsel.

He looked at the yard and noted it was swept and in good order and the house was as neat as a new pin. But what was hidden behind the door of the lumber room? After dinner he spoke to the young woman.

"I have a request," he stated. "Could I have permission to open the door to your lumber room?"

The young girl's face grew sombre as her cheeks reddened with embarrassment.

"No, it…it…is not to be opened," she stammered.

The young man's heart sank. How beautiful her eyes were, how tender her face. But the door to the lumber room had remained closed.

The young man took his leave without asking for her hand. His head hung low and his steps were heavy with regret as he left the house. But his father's instruction was very clear: he could not ignore it.

Soon he met another young girl more slender and prettier than the first. When she smiled, joy radiated from her face and her eyes glowed like the stars in the night sky. The young man was certain this was the girl for whom he had been searching.

He thought to himself, 'She is so pretty. If only Father could see her. He would surely approve of her and rejoice with me.'

Again the front yard was ordered and welcoming. Again the house was as neat as a pin. From the moment he entered the house, he thought he would ask for her hand in marriage, but restrained his ardent desire.

The young man was eager to put forward his request so shortly after dinner he asked, "May I open the door to your lumber room?"

He was sure his request would not be refused, but he was wrong. The door remained shut. The young woman declined with embarrassment.

With a broken heart the young man left the house.

"Will I ever find someone suitable to marry?" he asked himself.

He then met a third beautiful young woman and for a long time considered what he should do. He was irresistibly drawn to her as never before had he met a girl as kind and tender as she. But each day uncertainties grew deep in his heart as nagging doubts kept bothering his thoughts.

'I didn't know there could be such happiness in the world. I have never met a kinder, more pleasant girl than this. But, what if the lumber room door in her house remains closed to me?'

Misgivings continued to fill his heart.

'Father could have made a mistake. He wouldn't have wanted me to stay alone for the rest of my life. So what, it is just a door. And behind it only old furniture and things no one needs. What does it matter if they are dusty and scattered about or clean and neatly ordered?'

Eventually, he decided to visit the young woman's home and ask for her hand in marriage.

She was sitting quietly and her smile lit up the immaculate, well-ordered room. He could barely contain his excitement and was about to speak, when he remembered his father's words.

'Son,' they whispered, 'ask her to show you.'

He moaned in his heart, 'Oh Father, why do I have to do this?' But he knew his father had loved him and knew what was best.

"Will you allow me to open the door to your lumber room?"

The young man's words echoed heavily. He could already hear the answer. Yet another door would remain closed.

"I'm sorry, but that is impossible," the young woman's voice rang like a bell.

Her smile lit up more dazzling than ever, but the thickest darkness fell upon his soul. Had he been hit, he wouldn't have felt such pain. His heart was heavy with sorrow and ached as he stood to take his leave.

He paused in the garden, but before he could say good-bye to his hosts, the girl's father spoke, "You are a very odd young man. None of our guests have ever before asked such a thing. But even if they had, we could not have obliged."

Surprised, the young man hesitated. What could it mean?

Seeing the surprised look on his face, the young woman gently explained, "There is no door like this in our home, because we don't have a lumber room. When father was building the house, he said that if we live only with what we need, we wouldn't require a lumber room. So he didn't include one. We have nothing to put in it."

Oh, what joy filled his heart. She was just the kind of girl about whom he had always dreamed: kind, modest and sensible. How happy he was.

And at that moment he realized he had found the girl of his dreams only because he diligently followed his father's advice.

The Most Difficult Lesson

nce upon a time there lived a king who had only one daughter. She was the delight of his heart and filled his days with pleasure and purpose. Her presence seemed to illuminate the palace, but one of the things with which he was most impressed was her wisdom. When difficult decisions occupied his mind and heart, he often asked her for advice. She would always find the right words and the right solution to help him.

The princess was becoming a young woman and as she grew, her wisdom increased. Her reputation had spread throughout the neighboring kingdoms and every prince wanted to ask for her hand in marriage. But the king did not know which one to choose.

"My dear," he addressed his daughter one day, "I need your help to make one of the most important decisions of my life. How can we choose the one who will become your husband?"

"Father, I will willingly marry the prince who can give the correct response to my question."

"I'll miss you so much, dear child, but I'll be happy if we can find a person who will appreciate you as you deserve."

The king smiled at her tenderly and gave his order for the princess' question to be made public.

An edict was proclaimed for the princes to arrive at the palace in one month to give their responses. But it seemed that even a whole year would be too short to find the answer to the princess' challenging question:

What is the most difficult lesson in the world?

Who could travel the whole world, walk every street, meet each person in order to find the answer? How could the most difficult lesson be discovered? The princess' challenge had truly baffled those who sought her hand in marriage.

The appointed time arrived and the princes stood in the throne room before the king and his daughter. Many of the princes bore with them chests encrusted with gold and precious stones.

The princess took a small box from the table beside her and addressed her noble guests.

"In my hands I hold the answer to my question. I will marry the one whose answer matches the one within this box."

She replaced the box on the table. Minute by minute the guests became more excited.

The first prince to stand before the princess was from the neighboring kingdom. He began to speak.

"Your Highness, each ruler has fought against his enemies and everyone knows how difficult it is to lead a battle. But the greatest enemy to overcome is a person's own fear. Those who know how to conquer their fear have learned the most difficult lesson."

The princes nodded their heads thoughtfully. That really was a difficult lesson to learn. But was there anything more difficult than that?

Everyone's eyes were directed to the next prince. He stepped forward, removed the crown from his head and took servant's clothes from the chest beside him.

"It's nice to wear a crown and fine clothes," he said, "but in order to be a genuine ruler, you need to learn that you are no greater than those whom you govern. It is only when you serve the people that you fulfil the task for which you have been enthroned. The most difficult lesson is the lesson of humility."

Expressions of surprise and admiration passed across the faces of those present. Oh, that would be so difficult; an almost unachievable lesson. This could be the right answer, but was there anything more difficult than that?

One after another, the princes opened their chests and used the contents to illustrate what they considered to be the correct answer. Until, just two princes remained. One opened a beautiful casket studded with precious gems. He took out a sharp dagger and made a bow to the princess.

"Your Highness, every person learns difficult lessons throughout their lives, but the most difficult one passes through the heart. This is the dagger with which my adversaries tried to kill me. There is nothing more difficult than to forgive those who do you harm. To love your enemies is extremely difficult, but those who learn the lesson of love have learned the most difficult lesson in the world."

The king really was nonplussed. He had before him so many wonderful young men, each of them worthy of his daughter's hand. He looked at her. What was she hiding behind her calm face, behind her slight smile? Which of them had guessed what he did not yet know?

The last prince approached holding a small box in his hands.

"Your Majesty," he addressed the king, "my answer is inside this box. I kindly ask you to read it. If my answer is the same as that of the princess, I will be willing to ask for her hand in marriage."

The most difficult lesson is the one you have not yet learned.

The most difficult lesson is the one you have not yet learned.

Hushed, excited whispers immediately spread throughout the throne room as the prince placed his box on the table next to the princess' box.

The king approached the table and opened both boxes. A small piece of paper with finely written letters was lying at the bottom of each. There, the words were exactly the same:

The most difficult lesson is the one you have not yet learned.

All those in the throne room were astounded. Oh how true these words were. The lessons of courage, humility and love are exceedingly difficult, but everyone understands that when you learn your lesson, it is no longer difficult for you. What really is difficult is the lesson you have not yet learned.

The king was happy. An astute prince was standing before him and he was as wise as his daughter.

The prince knelt before the princess.

"Your Highness, we need courage to start learning and humility to admit that there are some things we do not know. But we need love to support us as we continue our way forward, no matter how difficult the path. Will you do me the honour of being by my side during the course of the difficult lessons I must learn until the end of my days?"

The princess was overjoyed. There were so many difficult lessons she herself had not yet learned. But over the course of the years, she would happily share her life with a husband for whom there was no more difficult lesson than that which had not yet been learned.

The Mirror of Desires

Many, many years ago, a king ruled over the most powerful kingdom in the world. His lands extended from horizon to horizon and he possessed unimaginable riches.

The king had only one son who longed to be married. But the prince had a very difficult problem to solve. How could he find a wise and sensible maiden who would marry him for himself and not for his untold riches? The prince pondered his dilemma for a long time, even consulting his father's advisors until, one day, he came to a solution. He would set a task for the young women to accomplish and marry the one who was successful in achieving the task.

Throughout the kingdom and further into the near and distant lands, an edict was proclaimed that the prince was searching for a wife. All the young women of the kingdom, as well as the neighboring kingdoms, were invited to the palace. The edict stated that each must be accompanied by a person she loved very much.

The day drew near and many excited young ladies began to arrive at the palace with their beloved chaperons. There were noble princesses, baronesses and duchesses, as well as girls from the villages and towns who had always dreamed of becoming a princess.

The clock ticked to the appointed time. The herald sounded and the king's chancellor announced the commencement of the proceedings and invited the young women and their escorts into the throne room.

As the prince rose from his throne, the room became hushed. He gestured to a carved wooden door to the left of the great hall.

"Your task is simple," he explained, "behind this door is a room within which is a mirror. Each of you may enter the room and stay for just one hour. When the time has passed, your companion will call you. The one who leaves the room immediately will become my wife."

The young ladies whispered.

"Oh, is that all?"

"All I need to do is stand in front a mirror for one hour?"

"How easy it will be to become the world's richest princess."

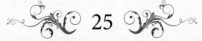

The first young woman, a very beautiful princess from a distant land, entered the room. The door closed softly behind her as her eyes were instantly drawn to her reflection on the opposite wall. She stood for a moment and was surprised to see the surface of the mirror move and an astonishing scene appeared.

There in the mirror the princess saw herself in a magnificent ballroom full of noble guests. She was dressed in an elegant ball gown and was dancing to the accompaniment of wonderful music. And oh, the prince himself was reaching out his hand to her. Everyone was admiring and applauding her during the never-ending ball.

Just as the next dance was about to start, she heard the voice of the chancellor, "Excuse me, Your Highness," he bowed his head, "your time is up. You must leave the room."

"But, but why? I only just came in."

The spellbound princess became flustered and did not want to leave the room or take her eyes from the enchanting scene before her.

As they were led away from the room, her mother attempted to assure her daughter that she had been called many times to leave the room. The princess did not hear even one word.

One after another, each princess entered the empty room, but not one managed to leave at the allocated time.

The next young woman to enter the room was the daughter of a duke. She stood in the center of the room and gazed into the mirror where a great gallery filled with indescribable riches materialized before her eyes. There were beautiful cedar boxes overflowing with precious stones and diamonds and pearls. There were fine marble statues, golden candlesticks and crystal vases. How could she look away, when there, in the middle of all the extravagance, the young woman saw herself in the most exquisite gown sparkling with pale pink gems? She had never dreamed of anything so glorious. Oh, if only the others could see her now.

Long after the hour was past, the chancellor gently escorted her from the room. She too failed to leave on time because she could not hear her father's voice.

For many days, the noble women and the maidens from the towns and villages made their way to the castle. They entered the room, one by one. And one by one, each left the room later than the appointed time.

Finally, one young girl was left standing at the entrance to the room. She could not understand why the others had failed such a simple task, but no matter what the cost, she was determined to leave the room on time. The girl's plan was to close her eyes and not open them until she could hear her mother's voice.

Even before stepping through the doorway of the room her eyes were tightly closed. The young girl stood there as the minutes passed so slowly, so tortuously, as if each one was a year. But she knew she must persist.

At last, when her determination was almost gone, she heard the familiar voice of her mother.

"I did it! I did it!" she exclaimed reaching for the doorknob to leave the room.

But just as she was about to turn the handle, the girl started to wonder, 'What is so special about the mirror?'

It took but a fleeting glance and she was immediately captivated by the scene: the vast array of the earthly riches of the prince. The vision was irresistible.

Even as the door opened and the chancellor asked her to come out, the girl could not withstand the lure of what she could see.

"But, I...I only looked at it for a moment."

The young girl was bewildered. In fact, the appointed time had long since passed and, in vain, her mother had continued to call her.

The prince was saddened that no young woman suitable to be his wife had been found.

He stood to announce the end of the reception. Suddenly, the doors to the throne room opened to admit a maiden accompanied by a simple, yet dignified, old man. They walked forward and stood before the prince.

The young maiden curtsied respectfully, "Your Highness, I have come to try the task you have set."

The prince explained the requirements of the test and said to the father, "When the hour has passed, you must call your daughter to come out of the room."

"My father can't speak, Your Highness," the maiden responded quietly.

Surprised, the prince asked, "Then how will he call you?"

"It will be enough for me just to hear his knock on the door," she assured him.

Murmurs and whispers filled the great room. Is that really possible? So many loud voices had remained unanswered. It was unbelievable that a light knock could bring someone from the room.

The chancellor ushered the maiden into the room then closed the door. She was surprised to find the room empty except for the large mirror on the wall. There was no table, no dresser, not even a chair on which to sit. How could a whole hour be spent in here?

The young maiden looked into the mirror and saw her dark hair, braided in heavy plaits, fall over her shoulders. She saw her new dress that fitted very well. She looked around the room and found nothing to do but wait patiently by the door and listen for her father's knock.

When the hour had passed, the maiden heard the light knock and straight away turned the knob, opened the door and stepped out into the bright lights of the throne room.

Everyone in the room gasped in amazement. The prince could hardly believe his eyes.

"Please tell me, what did you see in the mirror?" he asked, his voice trembling.

The maiden was surprised. "But what could I see there, if not myself?"

"Yes, of course, that is what every other mirror would show you, but this mirror is different. In this mirror, people see themselves as they desire to be."

"I have never desired to be anything more than I am, and I'm happy to be just as I am," the young maiden responded. "It was my father who insisted we come here so, to please him, I agreed." She turned and smiled lovingly at her dear father who was standing quietly by her side.

The prince could feel his heart growing in admiration for this pretty young woman. How happy he was. He knelt before her.

"If you marry me, your life will be very different." he said. "I have untold wealth which will be yours. But I want a wife who will love me even if I have nothing in the world. So if your desires begin to seize your heart and try to tear you away from me, please, come to this room. Stay alone in front of the mirror and don't let those desires drown out my voice."

To the very end of her days, even after she became queen, she would often stand quietly in front of the mirror and see that her heart's one desire was to hear the prince's whispering voice of love. And she would always leave the room before the surface of the mirror had the chance to stir.

Little Bear's Path

Little Bear and Little Deer spent most afternoons together. They had become inseparable friends after the incident in the forest when Little Bear had fallen into a deep, dark pit. Little Deer had run to Father Bear for help.

During the holidays, they were together all day long. They would play together in the glade or go down to the brook. There, Little Bear would find some of his favorite wild strawberries while Little Deer would forage on the lush grass and drink the clear water from the stream.

Little Bear's house was at one end of the glade and Little Deer's house was at the other end. Little Bear would cross the glade, walking along a path through the grass while Little Deer would stamp his little hooves along the path from the other side. They would meet in the middle. Sometimes they would visit Little Dear's house, sometimes Little Bear's, or they would continue together on their way to the brook.

One day, however, Little Bear reached the middle of the glade, but did not find his friend there. He looked down the path for a long time, but Little Deer could not be seen.

"What could have made him late?" he asked himself as he ran to Little Deer's house. It was quiet and lonely. There was no one around, so he returned home alone without meeting his friend.

Day after day Little Bear would run to the middle of the glade and peer along the path to see if Little Deer was coming, but there was no sign of his friend. Little Deer's hoof prints were gradually fading because the grass was growing thicker and thicker each day. The path to his house was gradually disappearing. Soon no trace of its existence would remain. Every day, Little Bear longed to run to Little Deer's home, but his little legs would not take him there. He was afraid of the empty house and the locked door.

One day, Father Bear asked, "Why are you not at the brook today?"

"Little Deer doesn't come to play anymore," Little Bear replied sadly.

"Is he ill?" his father asked, raising his head.

"No, he isn't," Little Bear sighed.

"Two days ago I saw him playing in the neighboring glade. Oh Dad, I was so happy to see him. I stopped and called out to him, but he replied saying he didn't have any time and we couldn't talk then."

Father Bear put his arm on Little Bear's shoulder and led him outside. "Come, let's take a walk. I'll show you something," his father said quietly.

Little Bear and his father walked along the path Little Bear had walked each day. The bees were humming around the greenery which was full of life at that time. They approached the middle of the glade and stopped. The familiar path had almost disappeared in the lush, dense grass. Little Bear sighed. There was now no sign of Little Deer's hoof prints. The grass swayed lightly in the gentle breeze as if stretching its hands forward reaching towards Little Bear's path.

Father Bear pointed towards Little Deer's house. "Look, what can you see?"

"I see a path that no one walks on," Little Bear murmured sadly.

"Yes, but it tells you much more. See where the grass is shorter and Little Deer's hooves have stepped. This makes me think of the past when someone has run to meet you. I don't know why he is no longer meeting you each day, but now, it would be difficult for him to reach where your path begins. Every day the growing grass will make his way even more difficult."

Daddy Bear spoke wisely.

Little Bear sighed again. "Dad, I can't keep coming down this path. It is too hard for me to go to his house day after day only to find it locked and empty."

"I know, Son. I don't expect you to do that. You only need to come to this point, to the middle. Your path will help you keep your heart open. It will be like writing a silent letter, little by little, every day, an out-stretched, guiding hand. Right now, Little Deer doesn't have time for you and he can't hear what you want to say, but the silent letter you write with your feet will be here waiting for him. Just don't let the grass grow on your path."

"But he may never come this way again, Dad!" Little Bear cried, lifting his head.

"Yes, that is possible, but if he does decide to come again to the glade looking for you, he will get to this point and realise that you haven't forgotten him. Then he will understand how much you love him. He will see that you've been waiting for him every day and your love for him will shine brighter than ever. Your path will make it much easier for him to find his way back to you."

Father Bear continued, "My dear son, don't let the grass on your path speak on your behalf as the grass on Little Deer's path is speaking for him."

Little Bear looked ahead of him. The green blades of grass, so fresh and young, were growing lush and had reached the very end of his path. Would he let the grass on his path grow and cover his own steps? Would he let that stop him from taking the path to the middle of the glade where no one waited for him? Was it worth the effort for someone who could not even find time to talk to him?

Little Bear's path, so dear and precious, had been filled with so much laughter and joy. And if he looked closely, he could just make out some of Little Deer's hoof prints: one here, another over there. These few faint impressions preserved his joy as Little Bear remembered the happy times he spent with his friend.

Then Little Bear decided that every single day he would walk along his path so the grass would not cover Little Deer's precious hoof prints.

He didn't know whether Little Deer would ever again run to meet him from the other end of the path. It was impossible to know. But Little Bear had his own path on which to walk while thinking of his dear friend, even though it might seem to become a little harder each day. The hoof prints would remind him of Little Deer and give him the strength to continue to the very end.

So Little Bear walked on. He wanted to keep his path untouched by the grass leaving a clear path to his home. And he would be patient. Little Bear was determined to make sure that someday, if Little Deer came to the end of his own path covered by grass, he would be able to find his way. And Little Bear would be ready, waiting for him with the warmest hug in the world.

To my wonderful parents, Spas and Lilka Nachev

Acknowledgements

I would like to extend my utmost appreciation to those who have helped turn this book into the quality product it has become – the translators of the original Bulgarian texts: Galina Dobreva and Emilia Handzhiyska; the editor of the English texts and her tremendous help: Marcia Patterson; the graphic designer: Rossen Antov; Diana Smilenova, a teacher who dreamed of seeing this series of books reach children throughout the world; the illustrators: Kate and Lilly Alexovs without whose eagerness this project would not have been possible. I also thank my husband who never ceased to encourage me. And last, but not least, I thank God who has always inspired me.

To contact with the author: preciousgiftseries@yahoo.com

WestBow Press books may be ordered through booksellers or by contacting:
WestBow Press
A Division of Thomas Nelson & Zondervan
1663 Liberty Drive
Bloomington, IN 47403
www.westbowpress.com
1 (866) 928-1240

Cover illustration by Kate Aleksova
Interior illustrations by Kate Aleksova and Lilly Aleksova

ISBN: 978-1-5127-2394-6 (sc)
ISBN: 978-1-5127-2395-3 (e)
Library of Congress Control Number: 2015920517

Print information available on the last page.

WestBow Press rev. date: 12/17/2015

Printed in the United States
By Bookmasters